E   Petach, Heidi.

           Goldilocks and the
             three hares.

$9.95   AUG 28 1996

DATE			

BAKER & TAYLOR

Hares to my agent,
EVELYNE JOHNSON!
It's her fault I did something bunny...er...punny.

Once upon a time there were three hares that lived in a cozy hole in the woods. There was a great big papa hare, a medium-sized mama hare, and a teeny tiny baby hare.

Hey, we're **rabbits**, not hares!

I know, dear. But maybe the artist doesn't know how to paint them.

HOME SWEET HOLE

Rabbits are cuter than hares.

Three **hares**?

Eh? Three bears?

Oh, I thought it was "The Tortoise and the Hare"!

Yes! Read that one instead!

Shh!

They each had a bowl for their oatmeal. The papa hare had a great big bowl. The mama hare had a medium-sized bowl. And the baby hare had a teeny tiny bowl.

So the three hares decided to eat out for breakfast.

...a pizza with mushrooms and extra cabbage!

The Three ~~Rabbits~~ Hares

8 Mice

Off they sped in their van. Meanwhile, a little girl named Goldilocks came bouncing down the forest path.

Actually, it's my **ball** that's bouncing down the path. Oops! Not anymore!
Her hair has a lot of bounce. Why don't we call her **Bouncylocks**?

She peered down the hole, but she couldn't see her ball.

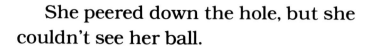

Wow, what a hole in the ground this place is!

Goldilocks? It's more like **Nosylocks**, if you ask me!

Let's tell the story of our laundry. We can call it "Moldy Socks and the Three Hares"!

In the kitchen of the three hares, Goldilocks found the three bowls—the great big bowl, the medium-sized bowl, and the teeny tiny bowl.

Hmm. Three bowls of burnt oatmeal.

Want to **bowl**?

Sure! What made you think of that?

Goldilocks tasted the oatmeal in the great big bowl. It was too hot.

YEOW!

Then she sampled the oatmeal in the medium-sized bowl. It was too cold.

Hmm. Ice cubes.

Hey! The illustrations are getting smaller with a lot of white space around them.

That's called "spot art."

The artist is showing a spot of laziness!

Laziness! You want to see more spot art?

Now look what you've done! I've got the measles!

Weasels?

Finally Goldilocks tried the oatmeal in the teeny tiny bowl. It was just right, so she gobbled it all up.

Then Goldilocks wandered into the family room and saw three chairs—a great big chair, a medium-sized chair, and a teeny tiny chair. First she sat in the great big chair.

The great big chair
was too hard to figure out.

So Goldilocks hobbled to the medium-sized chair.

The medium-sized chair went too fast.

Finally Goldilocks sat down in the teeny tiny chair. It was just right.

Then Goldilocks decided to see what was upstairs.

Upstairs, Goldilocks found three beds—a great big bed, a medium-sized bed, and a teeny tiny bed.

First she tried the great big waterbed. It was too hard to keep her breakfast down.

Next Goldilocks tried the medium-sized bed. It was too soft.

Finally she tried the teeny tiny bed. It was just right.

Soon Goldilocks was fast asleep.

As soon as the police arrived, they checked the kitchen.

Next they checked the family room.

An undercover investigation of the beds revealed more.

Huh? Oh, wow, what a dream I've been having! But I'm here now and you're here, Auntie Em and Uncle Henry and little Toto, too! There's no place like home, is there?
We're off to see the wizard!

Why is this page so white?

Well, I couldn't think of a background—so I drew a blank!

Well, look at that—there's the copyright information!

I thought they'd forgotten it!

It's long, but not forgotten!

Did they copy it right?

If they saved the jest for last, this must be THE END!

Not quite. Let's check out the back cover!

Checkers, anyone?

Library of Congress Cataloging-in-Publication Data
Petach, Heidi.
Goldilocks and the three hares / by Heidi Petach.   p.   cm.
Summary: Presents a contemporary takeoff
on the familiar folktale.
[1. Rabbits—Fiction. 2. Humorous stories.]
I. Goldilocks and the three bears. II. Title.
PZ7.P44132Go 1995 [E]—dc20 94-24495 CIP AC

ISBN 0-399-22828-4   B C D E F G H I J